By Ellen MacGregor

Illustrated by Paul Galdone

Miss Pickerell
and the
Geiger Counter

A TAB BOOK

Published and distributed by TAB Books, Inc., an Affiliate of
Scholastic Magazines, 33 West 42nd Street, New York 36, N. Y.

☆ ☆ ☆

To

ANN and ED CLARK

CONTENTS

1. MR. LYNCH MAKES A DISCOVERY

HALFWAY between the wide green banks of Square Toe River, a large steamboat chugged steadily downstream, kicking up a white froth of foam on the sunny brown surface of the water.

It was half-past ten in the morning.

Miss Pickerell came hurrying out of her stateroom, climbed briskly up a steep stairway to the top deck of the boat, settled herself in an empty deck chair, and took her crocheting out of the pocket of her pink sweater.

Through a narrow white railing in front of her, Miss Pickerell could look down to the lower deck of the steamboat, where a portable canvas swimming tank had been set up in the sun, in case any of the passengers felt like going swimming.

The only passengers who felt like it this morning were

1

two boys. They had yellow hair and were wearing bright green swimming trunks.

When they saw Miss Pickerell, they waved up at her.

"Did you ever see such a spectacle!" said a man in a gray suit who was standing beside Miss Pickerell's deck chair. "All that splashing!"

"Why, they're not splashing!" Miss Pickerell said. "They never splash when they swim. They're my nephews, so I ought to know. Their names are Homer and Harry. Homer and Harry are spending the summer with me."

"I beg your pardon," said the man in the gray suit, bowing toward Miss Pickerell, and tipping his hat slightly. "But I wasn't talking about—"

"We're on our way to the state capital where the circus is going to be," Miss Pickerell said. "Homer and Harry are going to see the atomic-energy exhibit, too. There's an atomic-energy exhibit at the state capital."

"I wasn't talking about Homer and Harry," the man said. "I didn't mean them. I meant out there."

Miss Pickerell shaded her eyes and looked where the man was pointing—out across the wide brown surface of the river.

"I don't see anything," she said, "except that low white building on the edge of the river that looks like a scientific laboratory, and has a helicopter coming down beside it."

"That's an atomic-energy experiment station," the

man said. "But don't you see? All that splashing up ahead of us?"

Miss Pickerell squinted up her eyes from the sun.

"Oh!" she said. "You mean that man in the bright blue rowboat. He certainly is splashing a lot! He must be in a hurry to get across the river."

"He'll *never* get across," said the man, "rowing like that. He's probably never even been in a rowboat before. He's probably a prospector."

"Why, that's ridiculous!" Miss Pickerell said. "He won't find any rock formations around here." Miss Pickerell knew a good deal about rocks. She had one of the finest rock collections in that part of the country, and her special collection of red rocks from the planet Mars had once won a gold medal at the state fair.

"For uranium, I mean," said the man.

"Why, that's even more ridiculous!" Miss Pickerell said.

The man pursed up his lips, as if he were trying to decide whether to say something else. Then he spoke.

"Apparently, Madame," he said, "you have not heard the mysterious rumors about uranium deposits along the banks of Square Toe River."

"If anybody ever found any uranium around here," Miss Pickerell said, "I'd be very much surprised. Uranium is found in rocks. And anybody could tell just by looking that this isn't rocky country. For one thing, the banks of the river are flat. That means they have been

built up by fine particles that were carried downstream
in the river when there were floods, and then dropped
when the water went down. Rocks are too heavy to be
carried in the water that way."

Miss Pickerell knew quite a bit about geology, from
her study of rocks. She knew how rivers, and winds, and
even ocean waves, are always gradually wearing the
land away in one place, and building it up in another.

"I'm just telling you what I've heard," said the man.

"The only possible way uranium might be discovered
around here," Miss Pickerell said, "would be by drilling
deep into the earth. If you drill deep enough into the
earth, you always come to rocks. But even then, they
might not be the kind of rocks that had uranium in
them."

Miss Pickerell stopped talking because she could see
the man wasn't paying any attention to her. He was still
watching the awkward efforts of the man who was trying
to row across the river. The steamboat was now almost
opposite the rowboat.

"Such a spectacle!" the man said again. "Do you mind
if I sit down in this empty deck chair beside you?"

"Not at all," said Miss Pickerell, continuing with her
crocheting. She was crocheting belts for Homer and
Harry out of bright red plastic cord.

The man beside her seemed so upset by the way the
boat was being rowed that Miss Pickerell decided he
must be a rowing instructor. She asked him if he was.

"Indeed no!" said the man. "My name is Cornelius Lynch, and I happen to own this Square Toe River steamboat. Every so often I take a trip myself—sort of a personal inspection trip. And it's a very good thing I do. Do you know what I discovered yesterday? Do you know what I discovered somebody had brought on board this ship yesterday when it stopped in Square Toe City? Somebody has brought a—"

Behind them the steamboat whistle blew so loudly and shrilly that Miss Pickerell almost jumped out of her deck chair.

"You do expect your boat to be on time, don't you, Mr. Lynch?" she asked. "I mean about getting to the state capital by five o'clock this afternoon? It's very important."

"Only an emergency could make us late," said Mr. Lynch. "Would you care for a piece of peppermint candy?"

Miss Pickerell was very fond of peppermint, and her mouth began to water even before she put the piece of peppermint candy into her mouth.

"You mentioned the circus in the state capital," Mr. Lynch said. "I presume you and your nephews want to get there in plenty of time for the evening performance?"

"That isn't the reason we are making this trip," Miss Pickerell said. "Homer and Harry will see the circus, of course. They're also going to the atomic-energy exhibit.

But we wouldn't have come at all, except that I have an appointment with Dr. Haggerty."

"You're not ill!" said Mr. Lynch, leaning forward in concern. "Perhaps I shouldn't have offered you—"

"No, no," said Miss Pickerell. "Dr. Haggerty isn't a doctor for people. He's a veterinarian. Dr. Haggerty is the circus veterinarian."

"I don't think I quite understand," said Mr. Lynch, with a frown.

"Of course I could have taken my cow to the veterinarian in Square Toe City," Miss Pickerell said. "But she already knows Dr. Haggerty and likes him. And he was kind enough to agree to see her at the circus today, right after the afternoon performance, so—"

"Do you mean to tell me," said Mr. Lynch, jumping to his feet, "that you are the person who brought a cow on board this ship yesterday in Square Toe City!"

"I never would have," Miss Pickerell said, "if I had known where your sailors were going to put her."

"It's distinctly against our regulations," said Mr. Lynch, "to have a cow on board this ship. Especially a sick cow."

"She's not sick," Miss Pickerell said. "It's just that it's time for her regular physical examination. I always like to see that my cow gets a thorough physical examination at least once a year. I am very fond of my cow, Mr. Lynch."

"That may be," said Mr. Lynch. "But regulations are—"

"I didn't want to come on your boat in the first place," Miss Pickerell said. "Except that Homer and Harry did. And it seemed more right to do what the majority wanted. But I wouldn't have come at all if I had known your sailors were going to put my cow down inside the ship, instead of letting her ride up on deck, where she could see what is going on. She could, just as well as not."

Mr. Lynch clapped both hands to his head and rolled his eyes up to the sky. Then he lowered his gaze and looked thoughtfully at the shore.

"Excuse me, Madame," he said, stepping carefully over Miss Pickerell's outstretched feet. "I've just had an idea. I have a plan."

"It's been pleasant talking to you," Miss Pickerell said politely, as Mr. Lynch tipped his hat and walked away.

If Miss Pickerell had known what Mr. Lynch's plan was, she wouldn't have been quite so polite.

2. MISS PICKERELL'S COW

MISS PICKERELL rolled up her crocheting, stuffed it in the pocket of her pink sweater, and went down inside the ship to see if her cow was all right.

Miss Pickerell had made so many trips down into the ship to see her cow, since they had come on board yesterday afternoon in Square Toe City, that she had no difficulty in finding her way.

She had even waked herself up every two hours during the night, so she could come down to make sure all was well.

At the foot of the last flight of iron stairs, Miss Pickerell had to go through a narrow passage which she thought must be right next to the engine room, because it smelled of oil and heat and was very noisy. The passage led her to a large, dimly lighted space with a wide metal

8

door that could be opened right in the side of the ship for loading and unloading.

At first Miss Pickerell could see only the top of the cow's head, because the center of the space was filled with a large pile of rocks of all different sizes, which Miss Pickerell had to clamber over, holding her skirts out of the way, each time she made one of her visits to the cow.

She supposed the rocks were used for ballast. When the ship had a light cargo, the rocks would add weight, and keep the ship at the proper depth in the water.

If she had not been so concerned about her cow, and if it had not been so dark down here, Miss Pickerell would have been tempted to stop and examine the rocks. She was always interested in finding new specimens for her rock collection.

The cow turned her head eagerly as Miss Pickerell approached, and Miss Pickerell heard the pleasant jingle of the silver cowbell that hung suspended from a leather strap about the cow's neck.

Miss Pickerell patted the cow and stroked her neck and spoke a few reassuring words to her.

In the dimness, she looked at her watch.

"It's almost eleven o'clock," Miss Pickerell said to the cow. "Only a few more hours and we'll be there. And I promise you I'll never take you on a boat again unless they'll let you ride up on deck instead of down in a dark old place like this full of rocks."

The cow mooed gently in response.

Far above them, the boat's whistle blew again, and the cow shuddered delicately.

Suddenly the dull thrum of the engines increased to a more rapid throbbing. The cowbell jingled sharply. Miss Pickerell heard a quick shuffle of hoofs as if the cow were adjusting her balance, and she herself felt a steady sideward pull as though the ship were changing its direction.

As fast as she could, without seeming too abrupt about it, for she did not want to alarm her cow, Miss Pickerell patted the animal good-by, and hurried up on deck to see what was happening.

3. A CHANGE IN PLANS

THIS TIME Miss Pickerell did not climb to the top deck. She hurried out onto the lower deck where Homer and Harry were still swimming in the portable canvas swimming tank.

Miss Pickerell made an unpleasant discovery.

"Why, the boat's turned around!" she said. "We're going back upstream!"

A white-coated steward came around just then with little cups of hot beef tea for all the passengers.

"Now, see here!" Miss Pickerell said. "I'm not going to stand for this! My cow doesn't have to put up with this! My cow has an appointment at the circus for 5:30 this afternoon. Where will I find Mr. Lynch?"

"Up there," said the steward, pointing over his shoulder with his chin, because his hands were holding the tray that had the little cups of hot beef tea.

Miss Pickerell turned around and looked up.

Mr. Lynch was standing on the upper deck, behind the narrow white railing, with his hands in the pockets of his gray coat.

"Will the passengers please pay attention?" Mr. Lynch said. "I have an announcement to make."

All the passengers crowded around the portable swimming pool. Homer and Harry stopped swimming and listened.

"There is going to be a brief delay," Mr. Lynch said. "Because we're going to make an unscheduled stop."

Miss Pickerell waved her hand. "You said, Mr. Lynch," she said, "that only an emergency could make us late."

"This *is* an emergency," said Mr. Lynch. "However, I think you'll find—"

"I have a cow on board this ship," Miss Pickerell said, "who is on her way to have her annual physical examination. She isn't sick now. But she *might* be, if she has to ride down in that dark old hole much longer."

"May I remind you, Madame," said Mr. Lynch, "that your cow is on board this ship in distinct violation of our regulations? And that brings me to what I was going to say. Now—"

"Besides," Miss Pickerell said, "it wouldn't be polite to be late. It wouldn't be polite to Dr. Haggerty when he has been kind enough to arrange to see us right after the afternoon performance."

"If that's all you have to say, Madame," Mr. Lynch said, "I'll continue. Now, I have just had a telephone conversation on our ship-to-shore telephone, and—"

"I think it's very inconsiderate," Miss Pickerell said, "of whomever you were talking to, to want you to make an unscheduled stop. It might be very important for someone on the boat to get to where they were going on time. Like my cow. Perhaps you could call them back, Mr. Lynch, on your ship-to-shore telephone, and explain."

Mr. Lynch took his hands out of his pockets and clenched them on the narrow white railing in front of him.

"You will notice, Madame," he said, "that this boat is now headed toward a place on the riverbank where there is a small town. A railroad runs through this town. I have just learned, from my telephone conversation, that at two o'clock this afternoon there will be a train to the state capital where the circus is. If you would be good enough, Madame, to remove your cow from this ship—where she has no business being in the first place —and proceed the rest of your way by train, we will be more than glad to refund your entire fare."

"That's very kind of you," Miss Pickerell said. "I wouldn't want to put you to the inconvenience of stopping there, except that it *is* rather important."

"It's not a question of convenience," Mr. Lynch said. "It's a question of regulations. It's against regulations to

have a cow on board this ship. I shall give orders to have
the gangplank put out the minute we stop."

"What about us?" Homer asked. He and Harry had
been standing in the middle of the swimming pool, lis-
tening.

"Yes," said Harry. "Do we have to get off too?"

"You can stay on the boat. Or you can go with your
aunt," Mr. Lynch said. "That's entirely up to you."

"Well, not quite," Miss Pickerell said. "I'm responsible
for Homer and Harry." And she motioned to them to get
out of the swimming pool.

Mr. Lynch said, "I would advise you and your
nephews to go to your staterooms and pack your things
immediately."

4. MISS PICKERELL GOES ASHORE

WHEN Miss Pickerell came out of her stateroom, after packing her things, she almost bumped into Homer and Harry who were waiting for her, right outside the door. They had got dressed, and were wearing bright orange T shirts and blue jeans.

"I've decided," said Miss Pickerell, "that you don't have to come with me." She had her hat on, and she was carrying her purse and the little straw satchel that she always took with her when she was traveling. "If you'd rather stay on the boat."

"Oh," said Homer. "But we've been thinking about it."

"Yes," Harry said. "We have."

"We've been thinking that we might look for new kinds of rocks for your rock collection," Homer said.

"Yes," said Harry. "While we wait for the train."

"This isn't the right kind of country to look for rocks

17

in," Miss Pickerell explained. "But thank you just the same."

"We found a new kind of rock for your rock collection in that cave on Square Toe Mountain," Homer said. "Don't you remember?"

"Yes," Harry said. "That yellow rock that had an arrowhead embedded in it."

"Well, that's different," Miss Pickerell said. "There are a lot of different kinds of rocks on Square Toe Mountain. But you wouldn't find any kinds of rocks in this type of country. Not even the most common kinds of rocks—rocks that have quartz, or mica, or feldspar in them."

She explained to them, as she had to Mr. Lynch, how the land on the wide riverbanks had been built up from tiny bits of soil carried in suspension in the water.

"When it rains upstream," she said, "bits of soil are washed down into the river. Some of them are so tiny that they don't settle on the bottom of the river. The movement of the water keeps them suspended." She moved over to the rail and pointed down at the brown water. "That's what makes the water so brown," she said.

"Oh," said Homer. "Well, if there won't be any rocks, I guess we'll stay on the boat."

And Harry said, "Yes. Let's."

"When the boat arrives at the state capital," Miss Pickerell said, giving them some money from her purse, "you go right to the circus. Go right to Dr. Haggerty's office . . . or whatever the circus has him use for an office. I'll be waiting there for you, if I get there first. If I'm not there, you wait for me. So none of us will get lost."

"Couldn't we wait for you at the atomic-energy exhibit?" Homer asked.

"Yes," said Harry. "Instead of at Dr. Haggerty's office?"

"Oh, I suppose so," Miss Pickerell said.

"We might be inside," Homer said.

"Yes," said Harry. "Seeing the exhibit."

"All right," Miss Pickerell said.

The boat's whistle gave a shrill blast. They had arrived. Miss Pickerell looked down at the rickety pier and the cluster of wooden buildings that made up the small town where she and her cow were to land.

Right below where Miss Pickerell and Homer and Harry were standing, the wide metal door in the side of the ship was pushed open with a creaking, crunching clang, and two sailors pushed out a gangplank and dropped it across to the little pier.

Miss Pickerell bade a quick good-by to Homer and Harry and dashed down all the flights of stairs to her cow in the interior of the ship.

"My cow will be *so* glad to get off," she said to the two sailors, who were busily shoveling a pathway through the rocks so that the cow could reach the opening.

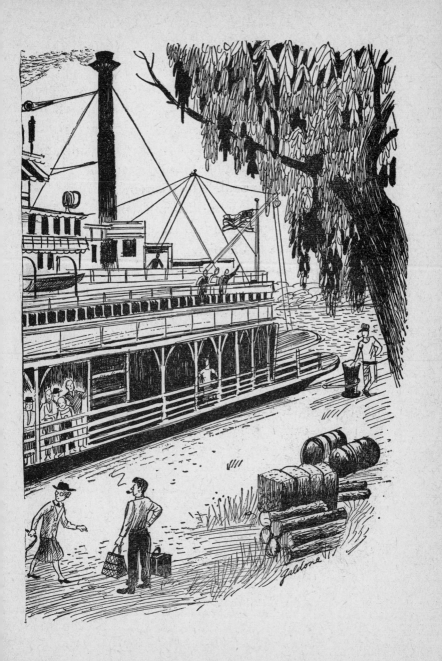

And then she was afraid she might have hurt their feelings.

"I know it wasn't your fault," she said. "I know you had to put her down here. I know you're supposed to observe regulations."

One of the sailors stepped out onto the gangplank and tested its strength by springing up and down on it.

"It's safe enough," he said. "For your cow."

The other sailor held Miss Pickerell's purse and her little straw satchel, until she had carefully led her cow across the gangplank to the pier.

Miss Pickerell thanked them both.

"Isn't it lucky there's a train to the state capital at two o'clock this afternoon!" she said. "I just hope there won't be any trouble about tickets."

5. TROUBLE ABOUT TICKETS

MISS PICKERELL was very happy when she saw how eagerly the cow welcomed her release from the dim dungeon on the ship.

As soon as they stepped off the pier, the cow made her way to a lush green field of grass on the edge of the river. She stood there grazing, lifting her head now and then to look back at Miss Pickerell as if to express her gratitude.

Feeling that the cow would be safe and happy there, Miss Pickerell set down her little straw satchel at the edge of the field and proceeded to make arrangements for their trip on the two o'clock train.

The little town had only one street, and as she looked up it from the landing pier, Miss Pickerell located the railroad station, set a little apart from the other buildings, at the far end.

Miss Pickerell was in such a hurry to see about tickets that she didn't pay much attention to the other buildings. In fact, she might have gone the whole length of the street without really seeing them, except that just as she found herself in front of a small general store with a little wooden porch in front of it, Miss Pickerell suddenly became violently hungry.

She entered the store and purchased some coconut macaroons and some peppermint pop.

The storekeeper was a kindly man with a gentle voice, and when Miss Pickerell asked if she might eat the macaroons and the pop right there, he insisted on carrying his rocking chair out on the little porch for Miss Pickerell to sit in.

Miss Pickerell was quite touched by his generosity.

As she tipped back her head to drink the last of the peppermint pop, Miss Pickerell noticed, for the first time, a small wooden building directly across from the store. It looked like a house, yet the door had a sign painted on it saying SHERIFF'S OFFICE. Miss Pickerell noticed that the blind in the front window was pulled down.

She supposed the sheriff must be away on official business.

Miss Pickerell turned in her pop bottle, thanked the storekeeper for his hospitality, and went on to the railroad station.

Only once did she turn around. That was when she heard the boat's whistle. Already the boat was some distance out in the river.

The station had a wooden platform, and Miss Pickerell's feet sounded loud on the wooden boards. The air inside the station smelled like smoke that had been there a long time.

Behind the ticket window, Miss Pickerell heard the clicking of a telegraph key. A man in a green eyeshade was sitting at a desk, filling out some forms with pieces of carbon paper between them. He was wearing arm bands to hold his sleeves up, so that his cuffs would keep clean.

"I'd like to buy two tickets," Miss Pickerell said.

The man at the desk continued to fill out his forms. He filled in two more lines and Miss Pickerell decided he hadn't heard her. Maybe the telegraph key was making too much noise.

She was about to knock on the ledge of the window to attract his attention, when the man said, "Where to?"

He put his pencil behind his ear, got up from his chair, and came across to the ticket window.

Miss Pickerell told him the name of the state capital.

"Full fares, or half?" asked the man.

"One ticket is for me," Miss Pickerell said. "We want to get there as soon as possible, on account of—"

"That'll be full fare," said the man. He took a long

green ticket out of a drawer under the window ledge, and began to write on it with a ballpoint pen. "And the other?"

"I'm not quite sure," said Miss Pickerell. "I've never taken her anywhere on the train before."

"What is the age of your traveling companion?" asked the man, as he continued to write.

"Ten," Miss Pickerell said. "She was ten years old two weeks ago last Tuesday. For a birthday present, my nephews, Homer and Harry, gave her—"

"That'll be half fare," the man said.

He took another long ticket out of the drawer and began to write on it.

"I wasn't sure," Miss Pickerell said. "She's used to traveling in a trailer."

The man began to fold the long green tickets. "This one's yours," he said. "And this one's for your child."

"She's not my child," Miss Pickerell said.

The man put the folded tickets into an envelope.

"She's more what you might call a pet," Miss Pickerell said.

The man, who had been about to give Miss Pickerell the envelope, took it back again.

"An animal pet?" he asked.

"Yes, of course," said Miss Pickerell.

The man opened the envelope and took out the little bundle. He unfolded the tickets and put one of them back in the drawer.

"She'll have to go in the baggage car," he said.

"Naturally," said Miss Pickerell. "You didn't suppose I'd try to take her in the train with me, did you?"

"You'd be surprised how many people do," said the man.

"I certainly am," Miss Pickerell said.

The man folded up her ticket and gave it to her in the envelope.

"You can check her on this ticket," he said.

"That's very kind of you," Miss Pickerell said. "But

I'm quite willing to pay a fare for her. She will take up quite a bit of room in the baggage car, I'm afraid."

"That might make a difference," said the man. "How big is she?"

"The average size," said Miss Pickerell. "She's a Jersey."

"A Jersey!" said the man. "A Jersey cow!"

"Of course!" Miss Pickerell said.

"Listen, lady!" said the man. "She's not going in the baggage car."

"You just said she was," Miss Pickerell pointed out.

"That," said the man, "was before I knew what the animal was. The animal cannot go in the baggage car."

"Will you kindly stop calling her 'the animal'!" Miss Pickerell said. "It makes her sound just like any ordinary cow."

"All cows are ordinary as far as I'm concerned," said the man. "If you want to go on the train, that's your business, but you can't take a cow with you."

"I have to get there," Miss Pickerell said. "My nephews Homer and Harry are on their way to the state capital. I have to meet them there. I'm responsible for them."

"All right, then," said the man. "Buy a ticket and go."

"You don't seem to understand," Miss Pickerell said. "I can't just leave my cow. Who would look after her?"

"You might try the sheriff," the man said. "He might look after your cow, if you paid him for it. The sheriff's always glad to earn a little extra money."

Miss Pickerell remembered the sheriff's office she had seen when she was sitting in the storekeeper's rocking chair, eating her lunch.

"I'm afraid the sheriff is away," she said. "The blind in his office window is pulled down."

"Very likely," said the man. "The train won't stop unless I flag it. And I'm not going to flag it unless you buy a ticket. Do you want a ticket, or don't you?"

"I'll let you know," Miss Pickerell said stiffly, and walked out of the station.

6. WHAT TO DO?

MISS PICKERELL didn't like to admit it to herself. But she knew the man in the station was right.

She would have to leave her cow behind. She would have to find someone to look after the cow while she went to the state capital to get Homer and Harry. But it would have to be someone who was kindly and understanding.

Miss Pickerell wouldn't think of leaving her cow with just anyone. And she wouldn't think of leaving her at all, except that she was responsible for Homer and Harry.

She was sorry now that she had agreed to meet them at the atomic-energy exhibit. If she had only insisted that they go to Dr. Haggerty's office, then she could try to call Dr. Haggerty by long distance and ask him to look out for them. But she couldn't expect Dr. Haggerty to leave the circus and hunt them up. Dr. Haggerty would have his own duties and responsibilities.

Miss Pickerell looked at her watch. If she was going on the two o'clock train, she shouldn't waste any time in finding someone to take care of her cow.

She remembered the kindly storekeeper. Perhaps he would be willing. Miss Pickerell stepped down from the station platform and hurried down the street to the store.

But just as Miss Pickerell reached the store, and had lifted one foot to climb up on the store's little front porch, she heard behind her a low moan, as if someone were in pain or great discomfort.

Miss Pickerell put her foot back on the ground. She looked around.

She noticed the sheriff's office across the street. The blind in the front window was still pulled down, but the door to the office was not quite closed.

It was through this door that Miss Pickerell again heard someone moaning, this time a little louder than before.

Her first impulse was to call loudly for the storekeeper. But the storekeeper might not hear her, or he might be busy, and after only a second's hesitation, Miss Pickerell made up her mind.

If someone was in trouble or pain, they might need help immediately.

She stepped to the door of the sheriff's office, pushed it open, and looked in.

7. SOMETHING IS THE MATTER
WITH THE SHERIFF

IT WAS a moment or two before Miss Pickerell's eyes became accustomed enough to the dimness so that she could see a man sitting behind a large desk with his head bent forward, and a white handkerchief held to his eyes. There was a notebook open on the desk before him, and he had a pencil in his right hand.

The man removed the handkerchief from his face, squinted up his eyes, and tried to write something in the notebook.

Miss Pickerell stepped into the room.

"You shouldn't try to write," she said, "if you don't feel well."

The man stood up, holding the handkerchief in his hand.

"I'm sorry," he said, "I didn't hear you."

He was a young man. A very tall young man, with a large silver star on his vest. He had bright red hair, cut close so it stood out all over his head, and Miss Pickerell thought he didn't look much older than Homer's and Harry's oldest brother.

The sheriff held out his hand. "I'm Burton Duval," he said.

Miss Pickerell said, "I'm Miss Pickerell." And they shook hands and said, "How do you do."

The sheriff said, "Excuse me, Miss Pickerell, if I close my eyes. I feel sort of funny, and the light seems to bother my eyes."

He offered Miss Pickerell a chair, and then he sat down at his desk again, rather weakly.

Something about the sheriff's eyes being sensitive to light, and the weak way he sat down, reminded Miss Pickerell of something, but she couldn't remember what.

The sheriff said, "What can I do for you, Miss Pickerell?"

"I thought maybe I could do something for *you*," Miss Pickerell said. "I heard you groaning."

"It was just that the light hurt my eyes," the sheriff said. "I expect I'll be all right."

"Well, then," Miss Pickerell said, rising, "I'll just run along. I have to ask the storekeeper if he'll take care of my cow." And she explained about having to meet Homer and Harry.

"It was very kind of you to investigate, Miss Pickerell," the sheriff said, "when you heard me. Perhaps you'd like to leave your cow with me. I have a barn right behind my office."

"Why, that would be wonderful!" Miss Pickerell said. "I'll go down to the riverbank and get my cow right now."

The sheriff cleared his throat. "There is just one thing," he said. "It's embarrassing for me to have to mention it, but there will be a slight fee."

"Well, naturally!" Miss Pickerell said. "I don't see why that should embarrass you."

"Because," the sheriff said, "it's so undignified. A sheriff shouldn't have to be renting his barn and doing odd jobs, just to get some money. A sheriff ought to receive a regular salary from the city. But *my* salary hasn't been paid for six months. Do you know, Miss Pickerell, that I sometimes even do baby-sitting! It's undignified for a sheriff! That's why I spend all my spare time prospecting for uranium."

Miss Pickerell started to tell the sheriff how unlikely it was that he would find any, but she didn't want to add to his troubles.

"I keep prospecting on the city's land," the sheriff said. "Especially the streets. The streets all belong to the city. If I could just find uranium, then the city could sell the ore to the Atomic Energy Commission, and they would have enough money to pay my salary."

Miss Pickerell refrained from reminding the sheriff that uranium didn't occur in this kind of country.

The sheriff stood up, hanging to the edge of the desk rather weakly. "Don't worry about your cow, Miss Pickerell. She'll be quite safe in my barn."

Miss Pickerell remembered now what the young sheriff's condition reminded her of. It reminded her of a time when Homer and Harry had been sick.

"Let me look at you, Sheriff," Miss Pickerell said gently. "Let me look at your face. And your hands and arms."

Then she said, "I hate to have to tell you this, Sheriff, but you have the measles."

8. A MYSTERIOUS DISAPPEARANCE

"BUT I can't be sick!" the sheriff said. "I can't be sick now. Not while I'm right in the middle of looking for uranium."

"Nothing is more important than one's health," Miss Pickerell said. "You should be in bed right this minute, Sheriff. Where's your bedroom?"

"In there," the sheriff said. He pointed over his left shoulder, and Miss Pickerell walked to the door he had indicated. Inside she saw a small, but cosy, bedroom with bright yellow roses on the green wallpaper.

Miss Pickerell lowered the blind and spread open the bed.

"Now," she said, when she had returned to the sheriff, who had sat down again, "I'll just go—"

"I almost have to keep on prospecting," the sheriff said. He turned his head in the direction of Miss Pickerell. "If I don't find uranium on the city's property, I don't suppose I'll ever get my salary paid."

"Well," Miss Pickerell said, "if that's all that's bothering you, Sheriff, you might just as well stop worrying about it right now. You'll never find any uranium around here. Unless you had the equipment to drill deep into the ground. And even then it would just be a chance."

"All I have is my Geiger counter," the sheriff said.

Miss Pickerell said, "I happen to know a good deal about rock formations, Sheriff. There are three main kinds of rocks. Igneous rocks come from hot lava flowing out of a volcano. Sedimentary rocks are formed from little pieces of other rocks that get worn away. Metamorphic rocks are made by heat and pressure inside the earth."

"I don't like to hurt your feelings, Miss Pickerell," the sheriff said. "I'm sure you know a good deal more about such things than I do. But still, there have been some very strange rumors about uranium here. People from outside keep coming in all the time to prospect. Just because of the rumors."

Miss Pickerell remembered the man in the blue rowboat she had seen this morning splashing frantically as he tried to cross the river.

The sheriff said again, "Of course you are probably right, Miss Pickerell. But if it *did* happen that there is uranium on the city's land, and I didn't find it just because I got sick and stopped looking, well. . . ."

The sheriff was trying so hard not to hurt Miss Pickerell's feelings, and it seemed so important to him to continue his prospecting for uranium that Miss Pickerell decided it would be unkind to continue arguing with him.

"I tell you what you can do, Sheriff," she said. "Just appoint somebody to be your deputy. Then you can send *him* out on the city's land to prospect for uranium. Now I'm going to go across the street and ask the storekeeper if he'll come over and help you get undressed and into bed. He seems like a kindly man. And he can call the doctor for you. As soon as I see the storekeeper, I'm going to go and get my cow and bring her back here to your barn. I want to see that she's comfortable before I go to the station to catch the two o'clock train."

"Maybe I could appoint the storekeeper," the sheriff said.

"I'd suggest that you appoint somebody else," said Miss Pickerell. "Your deputy might have to be away on official business. And if it was the storekeeper, he wouldn't be here to take care of you."

"Perhaps the man in the railroad station?" the sheriff asked.

"I certainly wouldn't appoint him, if I were you," Miss Pickerell said. "That man doesn't like cows. And it's my opinion that you can't trust a person who doesn't like animals. What you need for your deputy, Sheriff, is someone you can trust."

"What if I appoint somebody and he refuses?" the sheriff asked.

"He couldn't very well," Miss Pickerell said. "If you appointed a person, it would be that person's duty to be the deputy sheriff, I should think. Now I'll just run across and tell the storekeeper about you. And why don't you put some kind of a bandage over your eyes, Sheriff, to keep out the light?"

The storekeeper said he had had the measles, and he would go right over and help the sheriff undress and get into bed, just as soon as he had called the doctor. Then, later, after the store was closed, he would take his rocking chair across to the sheriff's bedroom and sit with him as long as the sheriff felt like having company. If the sheriff felt like eating something, he could bring it to him from the store, if the doctor thought it would be all right.

Relieved that the sick sheriff would be in such good hands, Miss Pickerell hurried down the street to get her cow.

She thought how fortunate it was that the sheriff had a barn where she could put her cow. Miss Pickerell looked at her watch. There would be plenty of time to get her cow comfortably settled, before she had to go and purchase her ticket.

Miss Pickerell reached the edge of the green field where she had left the cow and her little straw satchel.

She called to her cow, stooped over to pick up the satchel, straightened up again, took one step, and then stood stone-still, staring in frightened disbelief at the empty green field before her.

Slowly Miss Pickerell turned round, searching the riverbank in all directions.

Miss Pickerell's cow had completely disappeared!

9. THE NEW DEPUTY SHERIFF

MISS PICKERELL scarcely knew in which direction to look for her cow. Knowing her cow as she did, she was sure the creature would not have wandered off by herself. There would have been no reason for her to leave the green field of tall grass, even if she had been thirsty, because the river was right there, and the field sloped so gently that the cow could easily wade in with her front feet if she wanted a drink.

There seemed to be only one answer. Someone, for some unknown reason, must have lured Miss Pickerell's cow away.

As she thought about it, Miss Pickerell grew angry and resentful. But she was also frightened.

Something terrible might have happened to her cow.

Miss Pickerell started off upstream, only because she happened to be facing in that direction at the moment.

The cow could, she realized, just as well have been taken in the opposite direction.

After she had gone some little distance, with no sign of her cow, Miss Pickerell began to be afraid she should have gone downstream after all.

She was all ready to turn back when she heard, from the other side of a slight slope of ground, the gentle mooing of a cow.

Almost sobbing with relief, Miss Pickerell reached the top of the slope, and saw her dear cow lying in the shade under a weeping-willow tree, placidly chewing her cud. Behind the cow was the low white building that Mr. Lynch had said was an atomic-energy experiment station.

In her joy at finding the cow, Miss Pickerell did not at first notice that the cow was inside a sort of tent made of green mosquito netting, and that a fence of several strands of strong wire separated Miss Pickerell from the tent.

When she did make these discoveries, and realized that she was standing in front of a closed gate in the fence, there was no longer any question in her mind about how the cow had got here.

She knew now, definitely, that someone had put her here!

Breathing indignation, Miss Pickerell reached out to open the gate, and then she saw, for the first time, a sign saying:

AUTHORIZED PERSONNEL ONLY

TRESPASSERS WILL BE PROSECUTED
TO THE FULL EXTENT OF THE LAW

Miss Pickerell paused. Even in her haste to release the cow, Miss Pickerell paused, because she believed in laws. She knew they should be obeyed.

Regulations were different. Miss Pickerell sometimes felt that regulations were just made up by someone who sat down and thought them up. Regulations like not allowing cows on boats.

But laws were different. Laws were made by state legislatures, or by the Congress of the United States. And before a law was passed, it was debated and studied and thought about. And even then it didn't become a law unless a majority of the legislature thought it would be a good thing and voted for it. That's why Miss Pickerell knew that laws should be obeyed.

This sign said it was the law that only authorized personnel could enter. And although Miss Pickerell knew that someone who had no right to do so had put her cow here, she still didn't feel that that excused her from observing the law herself.

She wasn't quite sure who authorized personnel would be, but certainly a sheriff would be authorized. Or even a deputy sheriff. She would go back to the sheriff's office, and ask the new deputy sheriff to come and release her cow.

At first sight of Miss Pickerell, the cow had risen awkwardly to her hind feet, and then all the way up, jingling her silver cowbell. As nearly as Miss Pickerell could tell, at this distance, the creature seemed all right. She didn't appear to be frightened. She wasn't trembling.

The only thing was that the cow seemed to be switching her tail a lot. Miss Pickerell hoped she wasn't finding the flies too troublesome.

Back in the sheriff's office, Miss Pickerell knocked on the open door of the sheriff's bedroom. The sheriff had put a bandage over his eyes to keep out the light, and Miss Pickerell couldn't tell whether he was awake or asleep. He was wearing bright purple pajamas, and Miss Pickerell thought the room looked quite colorful and gay, with the sheriff's purple pajamas, his red hair, the white bandage, and the bright yellow roses on the green wallpaper.

"Who is it, please?" the sheriff called out. "You'll have to come in here."

"It's me," Miss Pickerell said. "I'm afraid I need the help of your new deputy, Sheriff. It's about my cow."

"I haven't made the appointment yet," the sheriff said, turning his head on the pillow, "but I'm about to. I've been thinking over what you said about what a deputy sheriff should be, Miss Pickerell, and I've decided on just the person. The person I'm going to appoint to be my deputy sheriff, Miss Pickerell, is you."

10. THE SHERIFF'S GEIGER COUNTER

"OH, DEAR!" Miss Pickerell said. "I'm sure that's very flattering, Sheriff. But it's quite out of the question."

The sheriff uncovered his eyes for a minute. "Didn't you say, Miss Pickerell, that you thought it would be a person's duty to be the deputy sheriff, if the person was appointed?"

"Well, yes," Miss Pickerell said. "But you see, I have a duty to Homer and Harry. I let them travel to the state capital by themselves. I'm responsible for them. I'm responsible for meeting them there."

The sheriff replaced his bandage. "I see what you mean," he said. "I'll try to think of someone else. I'll lie perfectly still and try to think."

"Will it take long?" Miss Pickerell asked, looking at her watch.

"It all depends," said the sheriff. "Sometimes when I lie perfectly still and try to think, I go to sleep. Then, of course, it takes longer."

Miss Pickerell wandered restlessly around the sheriff's office. Then she sat down in the swivel chair at the sheriff's desk and took her crocheting out of the pocket of her pink sweater. But she couldn't concentrate on it.

From the open door behind her came nothing but silence. Miss Pickerell had no way of knowing if the sheriff was still thinking, or if he had gone to sleep. She looked at her watch again.

Then she got up and walked to the bedroom door.

"Listen, Sheriff!" she said in a loud voice, just in case he had gone to sleep, "I'll be your deputy sheriff temporarily. Just long enough to go and get my cow." And she explained about where her cow was. "What are you looking for, Sheriff?"

The sheriff was rummaging under his pillow.

"Here," he said, holding out his badge. "You'd better put it on, Miss Pickerell, and wear it at all times, in case anyone challenges your authority. And thank you, Miss Pickerell, for taking over my duties."

"I'm not taking them over," Miss Pickerell said. "I'm only going to be the deputy sheriff long enough to go and get my cow."

"Raise your right hand, Miss Pickerell," the sheriff said.

"Why?" Miss Pickerell asked.

"So I can swear you in. Do you promise to faithfully discharge the duties of deputy sheriff?"

"I do," Miss Pickerell said. She pinned the silver star onto her pink sweater. "But just until I get my cow back."

However, half an hour later, Miss Pickerell was again sitting at the sheriff's desk, still wearing the silver star.

She had made a quick trip to the place where her cow had been imprisoned. She had released the cow and brought her back. The cow was now comfortably established in the sheriff's barn. There should have been nothing now to keep Miss Pickerell from going to the state capital to meet Homer and Harry.

The only trouble was that the train had already gone!

As she was putting the cow in the sheriff's barn, Miss Pickerell had heard the approaching rumble and roar of the train. And although she had run out into the street and started toward the station, it was too late. The train hadn't even stopped.

So now, much as she disliked having to bother Dr. Haggerty, it appeared to Miss Pickerell that she would have to make a long distance call to him at the circus and ask if he would find Homer and Harry, and take care of them until Miss Pickerell could get there, one way or another.

She was about to place the call, using the telephone on the sheriff's desk, when she observed a sign hanging from the neck of the telephone which said: OFFICIAL USE ONLY. Perhaps she had better ask the sheriff's permission first.

She turned around in the swivel chair and leaned back so she could see into the sheriff's bedroom.

The sheriff was lying perfectly still, and Miss Pickerell couldn't tell whether it was because he was trying to think, or because he was asleep. She decided not to disturb him.

To pass the time until the sheriff should speak, Miss Pickerell tidied the top of his desk, and dusted it with a large yellow feather duster she found hanging on a nail in the wall.

The notebook in which the sheriff had been trying to

write lay open on the desk, and Miss Pickerell couldn't help observing that it seemed to be a sort of log of his official activities. Many of the entries seemed to be careful notations about his search for uranium.

Miss Pickerell took the sheriff's pencil and brought the book up to date by adding brief details of the sheriff's illness, and mentioning that she was serving, temporarily, as the deputy.

The sheriff still hadn't moved, and Miss Pickerell once more took out her crocheting.

"When are you going to begin, Miss Pickerell?" It was the sheriff calling from the bedroom, and for a moment it startled Miss Pickerell, even though she had been waiting to hear him speak.

She leaned back in the swivel chair and turned around.

"Prospecting for uranium," the sheriff said. "When are you going to begin doing that?"

"Now, see here, Sheriff," Miss Pickerell said gently. "Don't you remember we went into all that before? There couldn't be any uranium around here. There aren't even any rocks. There aren't any rock formations here."

"But didn't you say, Miss Pickerell, that I could tell my deputy to prospect for uranium?"

Miss Pickerell remembered that she had said just that.

"Oh, all right," she said. "I'll go out and take a look around if it will make you feel any better. It won't take me long."

The sheriff cleared his throat.

"I don't want to seem rude, Miss Pickerell," he said. "I'm sure you do know a great deal about rock formations. But I wonder. . . . Well. . . . Just to make a more thorough search, would you mind using my Geiger counter, instead of just taking a look around?"

"Oh, all right," Miss Pickerell said, a bit grumpily. "Where is it?"

"In the bottom drawer of my desk," the sheriff said.

In the bottom drawer of the sheriff's desk, Miss Pickerell found a small black box, about the size and shape of a lunch box, with a round dial beside the handle; a pair of earphones with a long cord attached; some batteries; and a glass and metal tube, also with a cord attached.

Miss Pickerell had no idea if these were all part of the Geiger counter. She wished Homer and Harry were here. Homer and Harry knew a good deal about atomic energy, and they would be able to tell her about Geiger counters.

"I guess you'll have to help me, Sheriff," Miss Pickerell said, bringing the things into the sheriff's bedroom, and putting them on a table. "I've never used a Geiger counter before. Though, of course, I *am* familiar with the principle of the Geiger counter. I know Geiger counters detect radiations. I know Geiger counters are what you use for hunting uranium. Naturally."

"Geiger counters have other uses, too, Miss Pickerell," the sheriff said. "I'm going to take my bandage off for just a few minutes, so I can see what you are doing. Now, if you'll open the side of the box, you'll see there is a place to put the batteries."

"All right," Miss Pickerell said. "I've got the box open. Now I'm putting in the batteries. What do I do next?"

"Take off your hat and put on the earphones."

Miss Pickerell did so. She kept one ear uncovered, so she could hear what the sheriff was saying.

"Now plug in the cords," the sheriff said.

Miss Pickerell connected the cords of the earphones to sockets in the little black box where the batteries were. She also plugged in the cord attached to the glass and metal tube.

"That tube is the probe," the sheriff said, squinting up his eyes to see what Miss Pickerell was doing. "That's the part of the Geiger counter that is sensitive to radiations. You lay the probe on the ground to see if there is any uranium."

"If there *were* any uranium," Miss Pickerell said, "how would I tell?"

"There are two ways," the sheriff said. "That dial on the top of the box has a needle that swings around. But it's easier to listen with the earphones than to keep watching the dial. When there is uranium, you hear clicks in the earphones. Do you hear anything now?"

Miss Pickerell pressed both earphones to her ears, and then she almost jumped out of her skin.

"Why, Sheriff!" she shouted. "It clicked! The probe is lying right here on the table. And yet it clicked. Oh! There it went again! It clicked again. I can't understand it, Sheriff."

The sheriff motioned to her to remove one of her earphones.

"That's just the background radiation," he said. "It's called the background count. You always hear those little separate clicks. They come from cosmic rays out in space. You have to get used to the background count."

"Are the clicks from uranium louder?" Miss Pickerell asked.

"Not louder," said the sheriff. "Just faster. It's when the clicks start coming at a much faster rate than the background count that you know you have found uranium, or some other radioactive substance. I do hope you'll find some, Miss Pickerell."

Although Miss Pickerell knew the search was futile, she felt it was her duty to be thorough about it.

She went outside and walked down the street to the river. Every few feet, Miss Pickerell leaned over and laid the probe on the ground. Just as she had known, there was no change at all in the rate of the clicks. Nothing was registering except the scattered clicks from cosmic rays. Miss Pickerell pushed the phones back from her ears.

By this time, she had come quite close to the river and the little pier.

"I suppose I could listen just one more time," she thought.

But just as she had stepped forward a few feet, and was about to readjust her earphones, she heard behind her the thudding sound of running footsteps. She turned around.

A man, wearing a long white laboratory coat, like a scientist, was dashing across the green field with long leaping steps, heading straight toward Miss Pickerell. He had a small black mustache, and glasses with clear plastic rims.

"Can you tell me," he called breathlessly, "where—" And then he saw Miss Pickerell's badge.

"Oh, Sheriff!" he said. "Come quickly. We need a law-enforcement agent. There's trouble at the atomic-energy experiment station."

"Look," Miss Pickerell said, "I'm not really the—"

"Hurry, Sheriff!" the man said. "There's not a moment to lose."

11. TROUBLE AT THE ATOMIC-ENERGY EXPERIMENT STATION

AS MISS PICKERELL and the scientist hurried along the riverbank to the experiment station, the man introduced himself and gave Miss Pickerell a brief outline of the trouble.

"I'm Professor Perkins," he said. "And one of our test animals has disappeared. Right in the middle of a very important experiment."

Miss Pickerell, who was following close behind the professor, told him of course she was glad to do anything she could to help, but didn't the Atomic Energy Commission have its own law-enforcement agents? Didn't it have its own police?

"That's the trouble," said Professor Perkins. "Our experiment station doesn't belong to the Atomic Energy

Commission. We're connected with the state university. We do experiments with radioactive tracers. We buy radioactive tracers from the Atomic Energy Commission, and then we experiment with them."

"What kind of a radioactive tracer experiment were you doing on this animal?" Miss Pickerell asked politely.

"We're testing a brand-new kind of fly spray," the professor said. "Or we were before our test animal disappeared."

"What's the matter with DDT?" Miss Pickerell asked. "Why do you have to test a new kind of fly spray?"

"Well, it's a funny thing about DDT," the professor said. "But after a while flies build up a resistance to it. You can spray with DDT for two or three years and there won't be any flies, and then maybe the next year, the flies start to appear again, and DDT doesn't have any effect on them."

"Oh," said Miss Pickerell. She had noticed this same thing herself, now that she stopped to think about it.

"So," said the professor, "what we did was to apply this new kind of spray that we're testing, on one side of the animal, and then—"

"Why just on one side?" Miss Pickerell asked.

The professor explained. "That's so we could see whether the flies stayed away more from the side that had been sprayed, or from the side that hadn't been sprayed."

"It must have been pretty hard to tell about the flies," said Miss Pickerell. "Did you have someone on each side of the animal trying to count the flies?"

"No, no," Professor Perkins said. "That wouldn't have been necessary. Because we took some flies and put them in a screen box. Then we put in a tray that had a thin layer of syrup on it. The syrup had a weak radioactive tracer in it, and while the flies were eating the syrup, some of the radioactive tracer got on their feet, so that—"

"I think I understand," Miss Pickerell said. "Every time one of the flies lighted on the test animal it would leave a little spot of the radioactive tracer, and then all you had to do was count the spots by holding a Geiger counter—"

"Exactly," said Professor Perkins. "And that's why we used the fly spray on only one side. We wanted to see how many flies would light if no fly spray had been used at all. That way we could see how effective the fly spray was. If only half as many flies lighted on the side that had been sprayed, we could say the fly spray was 50 per cent effective. On the other hand, if *no* flies lighted on that side, the fly spray would, of course, be 100 per cent effective. Could you walk a little faster, Sheriff? There may not be a moment to lose."

Miss Pickerell tried to go a little faster, but she was getting rather out of breath.

"I must remember to tell Homer and Harry about

that," Miss Pickerell said. "I mean about always having something to compare your experiment with. You ought to tell other scientists about it, too, Professor. Such a good idea."

The professor said modestly that it wasn't his idea. "All scientists try to get something to compare their experiments with, if they possibly can," he said. "It's what's called a control." He was still walking very fast.

Miss Pickerell thought of something.

"I should think identical twins would be good for an experiment," she said. "You could do the experiment on one twin, and use the other twin for a control."

"You are absolutely right," Professor Perkins said, slowing down a little bit. "In fact, I have thought up the most interesting experiment to do on identical twins, in case any identical twins should ever come to the experiment station and volunteer."

Miss Pickerell told the professor about Homer and Harry.

"My nephews are identical twins," she said.

Professor Perkins stopped so suddenly that Miss Pickerell almost bumped into him.

"Oh, *do* you think you might be able to persuade them to come?"

"Certainly not!" said Miss Pickerell. "Didn't you just say you did experiments with radioactive tracers? That would be dangerous."

"No, no," said the professor. "Weak radioactive tracers

aren't dangerous. They are just strong enough so we can
tell they are there by using a Geiger counter. Please try
to get your nephews to come."

"Well, I don't know," Miss Pickerell said, "whether
they'd *want* to come." She was glad of a chance to stop
and catch her breath. She shifted the box of the Geiger
counter to her other hand. "And if they *did* come, they
couldn't stay for very long. They're only spending the

summer with me. They have to go home and go to school
again in the fall."

Professor Perkins took off his glasses and tapped his
teeth with them.

"Where are your nephews at the moment?" he asked.

"On their way to the state capital," Miss Pickerell said.

"I was just thinking," Professor Perkins said, "perhaps
I ought to interview them myself. Perhaps I could persuade them to come. Perhaps that would be more important than trying to find whoever it was that has stolen
the cow I was using for my fly-spray experiment."

"Cow!" said Miss Pickerell. "I shouldn't think people would let you use their cows for an experiment."

"Nobody let me use this cow," the professor said. "She was obviously abandoned. I found her in a field down by the pier. A beautiful fawn-colored Jersey."

"Professor!" Miss Pickerell shouted, and her voice quavered with anger. "That was my cow! She's in the barn behind the sheriff's house right now. And if you have harmed her in the slightest degree, I'll— I'll— I just don't know what I'll do!"

12. PROFESSOR PERKINS EXPLAINS

M ISS PICKERELL raced back to the sheriff's barn so fast, in her anxiety about her cow, that Professor Perkins could hardly keep up with her, even with his long, leaping steps.

"Nothing I have done has harmed your cow in the slightest degree," he said, panting.

Miss Pickerell did not answer. She only walked faster.

"Of course," said Professor Perkins, "I had no idea she *was* your cow. Or I wouldn't have taken her in the first place."

"You must have known she was *somebody's* cow," Miss Pickerell said.

"I assure you," the professor said, "you will find nothing wrong. However, if it would make you feel more comfortable to have her examined by a veterinarian, I'd be glad to—"

"She's *going* to be examined by a veterinarian," Miss Pickerell said. "Don't you worry about that!"

"What I mean is," said the professor, "I understand there is a very competent veterinarian connected with the circus. I'd be glad to try to borrow a cattle truck and take your cow to see him."

Miss Pickerell felt this was the least the professor could do, after taking such liberties with her cow, and she told him so.

"At the same time," said the professor, "I could interview your nephews. Usually, when I go anywhere, I go in the experiment station's helicopter. But we can't very well go in the helicopter, if we are taking your cow."

When they reached the barn, Miss Pickerell carefully examined her cow. As far as she herself could tell, the cow seemed to be unharmed. But it would be a comfort to have Dr. Haggerty's professional opinion.

"I suppose," Miss Pickerell said, "as long as you've already started your experiment, it wouldn't do any harm for you to finish it. But I'm going to stay right here with my cow while you do it." She handed the Geiger counter to the professor.

"I'm afraid it's too late now," the professor said. "Unless we started the experiment all over again. But I can try."

He put on the earphones, and held the probe close against the cow's skin, first on one side, and then on the

other, while Miss Pickerell stood close to the cow's head
and patted and soothed her.

"It's no use," the professor said, pushing back his earphones. "It's too late. The radioactivity is all gone."

"Well," Miss Pickerell said, "it couldn't have been very
good fly spray then. Not to have lasted any longer than
that."

"The fly spray is still there," the professor said, "but
we haven't any way of testing it now. The radioactive
tracer wasn't in the fly spray. It was in the syrup on the
flies' feet. And now it's all gone."

"I thought," Miss Pickerell said, "when things are
radioactive, they stay that way."

"Not forever," said the professor. "Do you think I
could use the sheriff's telephone? I think I know where I
can borrow a cattle truck for us to go to the circus in."

They went into the sheriff's office and the professor
called a number.

"The line is busy," he said, sitting on a corner of the
sheriff's desk. Miss Pickerell was glad she had dusted
the desk earlier. It might have got dust on the professor's
white laboratory coat if she hadn't. She noticed, through
the open bedroom door, that the sheriff was lying with
his face turned toward the wall. He must be asleep.

The professor was talking to her.

"The radioactive tracer we used on the flies' feet is a
kind that doesn't last very long," he said. "Half of it had

already gone in forty minutes. It was just half as strong after forty minutes."

Miss Pickerell asked, "Do you mean that radioactive tracers are sort of like electric light bulbs, except that instead of burning out all at once, they just keep getting dimmer and dimmer, until finally you can't tell they're there, even with a Geiger counter?"

"It's something like that," the professor said, "because some things have a lot of radioactivity, and some have very little, the way large light globes give off a lot of light, and small light globes are more dim."

"And after forty minutes," Miss Pickerell continued, "the radioactivity is half gone, and after eighty minutes it's all gone? Is that the way it is?"

"No, no," the professor said. "Everything that's radioactive has a *different* rate of losing its radioactivity. In some cases, it might be years before the radioactivity is all gone."

"What about uranium?" Miss Pickerell asked.

"The radioactivity of uranium is half gone in 4,700,-000,000 years. Uranium has a half-life of 4,700,000,000 years."

"That's quite a long time, isn't it?" Miss Pickerell said politely.

The professor went right on. "The radioactive tracer I used on the flies' feet had a half-life of forty minutes."

"Why don't you just say it's all gone in eighty minutes?" Miss Pickerell asked. "Wouldn't it be simpler than saying it has a half-life of forty minutes?"

"It would be simpler," the professor said, "but it wouldn't be right. It *isn't* all gone in eighty minutes. That's the funny thing about radioactivity. If something has a half-life of forty minutes, half of the radioactivity disappears in the first forty minutes. But in the *next* forty minutes, only half of what is left disappears. And in the next forty minutes, half of *that*."

Miss Pickerell was getting so interested that she almost forgot about wishing the professor would hurry up and try to make his telephone call about borrowing a cattle truck.

"Is that why uranium is so important for atomic energy?" she asked. "Because the radioactivity lasts so long?"

"Uranium is important," the professor said, "because it gives off such powerful radiations when enough of it is all together in one place. Uranium is naturally radioactive, but it is widely scattered through the earth. Ore that has uranium in it has to go to a smelter to get out the uranium. And even after that it has to be refined and purified. I'll just use the telephone again."

But the line was still busy.

Miss Pickerell opened her mouth. And then she closed it again.

"Yes?" the professor said.

"I had an idea," Miss Pickerell said, "but I guess it was silly."

"What was it?"

"Well, I just thought. . . . Maybe, if radioactive tracers keep losing their radioactivity at a certain rate, maybe they could be used in some way to tell how old things are. But that's silly, of course."

The professor rose from the corner of the desk and stood before Miss Pickerell's chair. He looked at her quite seriously.

"It's not silly at all," he said. "That's exactly the method archaeologists use. That's the way archaeologists now tell how old things are when they find buried ruins. They call it dating by the radiocarbon calendar. Radiocarbon has a half-life of 5,568 years. And anything that has ever been alive has had radiocarbon in it. By measuring the amount of radiocarbon that is left, it is quite possible to tell, almost exactly, just how many years old something is. Unless it's too terribly old. If anything is older than 30,000 years, the radiocarbon calendar doesn't work on it."

Miss Pickerell remembered something.

"Last week," she said, "Homer and Harry and I went on a picnic hike to a cave on Square Toe Mountain, and Homer and Harry found a new rock for my rock collection. They noticed there was a stone arrowhead embedded in the rock, and they wondered how long it had been there. Would the radiocarbon calendar tell how old the arrowhead was?"

"Not the arrowhead," the professor said. "Nothing made of stone. But if there had been a twig of a tree embedded in your rock, or a dead insect, or even if they had found an old sandal made out of straw—anything that had once been alive and growing—then it would be possible to tell its age by measuring how much radiocarbon was left. They do that with a very, very delicate type of Geiger counter. Oh, dear! Is somebody ill?" He had just noticed the door to the sheriff's bedroom.

Miss Pickerell looked and saw that the sheriff had got out of bed and had come to the door with an orange bathrobe over his purple pajamas. She got up quickly and made him sit down in the swivel chair. He still looked very weak.

"It's the sheriff," she said. "He has to keep his eyes bandaged because he has the measles, and his eyes are sensitive to light."

She introduced the men and explained that the professor was waiting to make a telephone call when the line wasn't busy.

The professor tried again, and this time he was successful.

"It's all right," he said, when he had hung up. "I can borrow the cattle truck. My friend will drive it over here and leave it. I'm going back now to the experiment station to change my clothes. I would feel a little silly going to the circus in my long white laboratory coat. I'll come back and get you and your cow in about half an hour, Miss Pickerell."

Miss Pickerell heaved a great sigh of relief. At last, after all this delay, she was finally going to get her cow to Dr. Haggerty.

13. THE SHERIFF'S SECRET AMBITION

RIGHT AWAY, as soon as the professor had left, Miss Pickerell told the sheriff about not finding any uranium. It was better than putting it off any longer.

"I'm really very sorry, Sheriff," she said. "But you know I did warn you. I told you it was impossible."

The sheriff asked Miss Pickerell where she had searched.

"All the way down to the river," she said. "I stopped every few feet."

"Well," the sheriff said, heaving a heavy sigh, "at least we *know* now that there isn't any uranium." And he told her that he himself had prospected carefully in every other direction. "If we hadn't been careful and thorough," he said, "if we hadn't looked just everywhere—"

"Sheriff!" Miss Pickerell said. "You talk like a scientist! Scientists talk about being careful and thorough." She remembered now the neat notations about uranium in the sheriff's official notebook.

The sheriff took off his bandage for a moment and blinked up at Miss Pickerell.

"Miss Pickerell," he said, "I'm going to tell you a secret. It's about my secret ambition."

"Why is it a secret?" Miss Pickerell asked.

"Because I couldn't ever be one," the sheriff said.

"Be what?"

"A scientist. Miss Pickerell, what I really would like more than anything in the world is to be a scientist—an atomic scientist, Miss Pickerell. But it's so impossible I hardly ever let myself even think about it."

"Why, it's not impossible!" Miss Pickerell said. "The town would just have to get another sheriff, that's all."

"It isn't that," said the sheriff, replacing the bandage. "It's impossible because I couldn't afford it. Even if the city did pay my salary for the past six months, I still wouldn't have enough money to go to college and study to be an atomic scientist. And besides that, I don't like to read books. Even when I was in school, I didn't. And scientists have to read a lot. Especially atomic scientists."

"A lot of people feel that way," Miss Pickerell said. "But they get over it when they start to read books about what they are interested in. Maybe you would too. It's never too late to begin."

"Maybe," said the sheriff, but he didn't sound very hopeful. "I feel a little weak, Miss Pickerell. If you'll excuse me, I believe I'd better go in and lie down again."

All of a sudden, Miss Pickerell remembered something. She remembered that she hadn't been quite truthful when she had told the sheriff just now that she had searched all the way to the river. Professor Perkins, with his appeal for help, had interrupted her before she had quite finished.

She knew, of course, that she would have no greater success than before, but she wanted to be able to say truthfully that she had been careful and thorough about her search.

And it shouldn't take long. She would have time to go and come back before the professor returned from changing his clothes.

Miss Pickerell put on the Geiger counter and went down the street.

14. AN INCREDIBLE DISCOVERY

MISS PICKERELL could tell pretty well how far she had gone before, because she remembered seeing her straw satchel almost opposite her when the professor had interrupted her.

She adjusted her earphones, and leaned down to put the probe on the ground. Nothing happened. Only the occasional clicks from cosmic rays.

She took three steps and tried again. Still nothing.

Three more steps, and again Miss Pickerell bent down.

This time, she almost jumped out of her skin at the shock of what she heard. There was a perfect fusillade of clicks clattering in her earphones!

Miss Pickerell stood up and slowly looked around. The soil here was no different from the rest of the riverbank, and yet, at this one spot—

Miss Pickerell picked up a stick and began to scrape

at the surface. Under a thin layer of soil, she came to a small rock.

There was no question but that this rock was the source of the radioactivity. Miss Pickerell tested it by holding the probe against it, and then farther away.

There was also no question in Miss Pickerell's mind, with her knowledge of rocks and rock formations, that the rock did not belong here. It was utterly unlike all the surrounding soil.

Still, if there was one rock containing uranium, there might be others.

Miss Pickerell checked the whole vicinity carefully but apparently there were no similar rocks.

Obviously this rock was here by accident. Someone might have dropped it here. Or thrown it. Perhaps someone passing on the river in a boat had thrown it.

This made Miss Pickerell realize that she had only checked the riverbank. She had not checked the river itself. She went out onto the pier, and even before she reached the end of it, even before she reached down as far as she could with the probe in the direction of the water, Miss Pickerell detected the increased tempo of the clicking.

There must be uranium-bearing rocks on the bottom of the river!

Miss Pickerell's first impulse was to run and tell the sheriff. He would be so excited.

And yet her own knowledge urged her to be careful. These rocks did not belong here. They had been brought here in some way. They couldn't have been washed down by the river because this river bed was old and flat. Only a river with a steep bed would have enough force to roll rocks along.

She returned to the rock in the ground and leaned over to pick it up.

There was something puzzlingly familiar about this rock. It didn't have an arrowhead embedded in it, and yet Miss Pickerell was sure it was the same sort of yellow rock that Homer and Harry had found for her in the cave on Square Toe Mountain. That rock was still in Miss

Pickerell's little straw satchel because she hadn't yet had a chance to study it since the day of the picnic.

With a leap almost as long as Professor Perkins', Miss Pickerell reached her satchel, picked it up, opened it, and took out the rock with the arrowhead in it. Her earphones clattered like hail in a hailstorm!

The two rocks were similar. They were both radio-active, and they were both yellow, with darker-colored streaks in them. The rock that had been lying in the ground had obviously also come from the cave in Square Toe Mountain!

But how?

And what about the rocks on the bottom of the river? How had they come there?

Suddenly a picture flashed through Miss Pickerell's mind—and she knew the answer.

In her mind, she was seeing again the pile of rocks for ballast inside the Square Toe River steamboat. She was seeing the two sailors using shovels to clear the way for her cow.

It was only too apparent what had happened! The steamboat must be using rocks from the cave for ballast. And whenever they needed to lighten the ship, to take on more cargo, they simply shoveled the ballast into the river. Probably no one had ever thought of prospecting for uranium in the cave on Square Toe Mountain.

But unless Miss Pickerell could stop them, the sailors on the Square Toe River steamboat might even now be shoveling some of the precious rocks into the river!

15. THE SHERIFF HAS TO HELP

"WAKE UP, Sheriff!" Miss Pickerell shouted, as she burst into the front door of the sheriff's office. "Wake up! Get up! We've discovered uranium!"

She dropped the two rocks onto the desk and reached for the telephone and held it with the mouthpiece up in front of her face. She took off the earphones and handed them to the sheriff, who emerged, pale and blinking, from his bedroom.

"This is Deputy Sheriff Pickerell," Miss Pickerell said to the operator. "I have to make an official call to Mr. Lynch on the Square Toe River steamboat on his ship-to-shore telephone."

"One moment please," said the operator, and while Miss Pickerell was waiting, she noticed for the first time a cattle truck parked outside the open doorway. Professor Perkins' friend must have left it.

She had only time to see the sheriff's look of rapturous astonishment as he put on the earphones and tested the rocks, before the operator said, "I have your party. Go ahead please."

"Mr. Lynch?" Miss Pickerell said. "I have something terribly important to say. Can you hear me?"

"It's against regulations," said the voice of Mr. Lynch, "to receive anonymous telephone calls on the ship-to-shore telephone. Who *is* this?"

"Miss Pickerell."

"Who?"

"Miss Pickerell. Mr. Lynch, please don't—"

"I don't think I know you," said Mr. Lynch.

"Oh, yes, you do," Miss Pickerell said. "You allowed me to go ashore this morning with my cow."

"Oh, it's you again, is it!" said Mr. Lynch. "I can't talk to you now. I have to find out how much cargo we're going to take on when we get to the state capital, so I can tell whether to unload the ballast or not. I'll have to ask you to hang up, Madame, so I can call—"

"Oh, please!" Miss Pickerell wailed. "Please don't!"

"I'm going to hang up now," Mr. Lynch said.

Miss Pickerell had an idea. Maybe Homer and Harry could do something to save the precious rocks.

"Please, Mr. Lynch," she said. "May I speak to my nephews, Homer and Harry? It will just take a minute."

"Sorry," Mr. Lynch said. "Against regulations. Good-by."

"Why, he's hung up!" Miss Pickerell said, as she looked at the sheriff and put the telephone back on the desk. "I couldn't stop him." And she quickly told the sheriff about the ballast.

She tried to call again, but this time the operator said the ship-to-shore telephone was busy. Mr. Lynch must be already calling the state capital to find out how much cargo there was going to be. If there was going to be a lot, he might give orders to have the sailors shovel out the rocks, even before the boat arrived!

"But there's one thing more I can try," Miss Pickerell said. "If I just get there in time. And, Sheriff, I'm afraid you'll have to help. Even if it does strain your eyes. Even if it does make your measles worse."

"Yes, of course," said the sheriff with quiet dignity. "This is an emergency."

Miss Pickerell went to the door.

"Call Professor Perkins," she said. "Tell him everything. Tell him I'm on my way. I'm going to drive his friend's cattle truck. Tell him to get out the experiment station's helicopter. Tell him to have it ready to start the minute I get there. Tell him how important it is, Sheriff. I've just got to stop Mr. Lynch from wasting all those rocks with uranium in them."

16. STOP! IN THE NAME OF THE LAW!

IT WOULD have been hard to tell who was the most surprised when, forty-five minutes later, the experiment station's helicopter swooped down beside the Square Toe River steamboat, and Miss Pickerell's face peered out through the transparent plastic bubble in which she and Professor Perkins were riding.

The two sailors who were shoveling rocks through the open door were surprised. Homer and Harry, looking down over the rail, were surprised. And so was Mr. Lynch, standing on the small top deck, his hands clenched angrily on the narrow white railing before him.

The helicopter rose. It hovered a moment above the ship while Miss Pickerell made sure that the portable swimming tank had been taken away so Professor Perkins could land safely. Then it settled gently to the deck, and

82

Miss Pickerell stepped out and looked up at Mr. Lynch.

Mr. Lynch opened his mouth to say that helicopters were against regulations on his ship, but Miss Pickerell raised one arm, pointed with the other to the silver star pinned high on her pink sweater, and shouted, "Stop! Stop that shoveling, Mr. Lynch! Stop it in the name of the law!"

Miss Pickerell had hardly finished explaining to Mr. Lynch about the uranium in his ballast, and he had hardly given orders for the shoveling to stop, when the ship-to-shore telephone began to ring.

All the way, from then till the boat reached the state capital, the telephone kept ringing.

News had reached the world about the new discovery of uranium. The sheriff had reported it. Newspapers and radio stations were all calling, all wanting interviews with Miss Pickerell on the telephone.

And one television station had set up a mobile studio right on the dock in the state capital, and as soon as the boat landed, Miss Pickerell was on television, with Homer and Harry beside her. She was only sorry that her cow couldn't be on television too.

In the interviews, Miss Pickerell tried to give the credit to the sheriff. It was all his idea in the first place, and anyway, she said, she had been acting as the sheriff's deputy, when she had made the discovery.

Homer and Harry were so excited and pleased about

Miss Pickerell's discovery that they invited her to go with them to the atomic-energy exhibit the next day. They invited Dr. Haggerty to go too, but he couldn't, because he had arranged to get a leave of absence from the circus so he could go to the sheriff's barn and examine Miss Pickerell's cow. He flew back with the professor, in the experiment station's helicopter.

At the exhibit, Homer and Harry explained so many interesting things about atomic energy to Miss Pickerell that she began to get interested herself. She made arrangements to visit an atomic-energy plant and took Homer and Harry with her.

At the atomic-energy plant, they learned about how things get to be radioactive—by being exposed to other things that are radioactive. Miss Pickerell thought it was a little like people catching the measles from being exposed to other people with measles.

They saw an atomic pile, or rather the shielding around it. They learned about the different uses of atomic piles, or nuclear reactors as some scientists called them. They found out that nuclear reactors can be used for power, or for heat, or for research, or to make radioactive tracers.

It wasn't until they were on the way home from the atomic-energy plant that Miss Pickerell realized she hadn't remembered to ask someone to explain to her just what atomic energy really was.

But Homer and Harry knew. And they explained it to her.

"Everything is made of tiny, tiny things called atoms," Homer said.

"Yes," said Harry. "And every atom has a tiny, tiny nucleus that's made up of neutrons and protons, and then there's a lot of empty space, and then there are some tiny, tiny electrons that keep scooting around the nucleus, going terribly fast."

"What makes an atom radioactive," Homer said, "is if its nucleus is shooting out neutrons."

"Yes," said Harry. "And if the neutron bangs into the nucleus of another atom, then *it* becomes radioactive."

"An atomic pile," Homer said, "or a nuclear reactor, is just a place where there is so much radioactive material that a great many neutrons are shooting out all the time."

"Yes," said Harry. "And what atomic energy is is just neutrons shooting out of atoms. That's all atomic energy is."

The Atomic Energy Commission made a survey of the cave on Square Toe Mountain and contracted with the people who owned it to buy all the ore they could produce. In a short time, over twenty tons had been mined, yielding 28 per cent uranium oxide. Because of this, the Atomic Energy Commission notified Miss Pickerell that she was entitled to the $10,000 bonus that they always gave anybody who found a completely new source of uranium if it was richer than 20 per cent uranium oxide. They explained to her that this bonus was to encourage people to look for new sources of uranium.

Miss Pickerell said she didn't want to be paid for discovering the uranium. It was a patriotic thing to do, and she was glad she had found it. That was all. And besides, she thought the sheriff ought to get the bonus. It was all his idea in the first place.

But the Atomic Energy Commission said they had to give the bonus to the person who had made the discovery.

Then Miss Pickerell remembered the sheriff's secret ambition, and suddenly she knew what she was going to do with the $10,000 bonus from the Atomic Energy Commission. She would establish a scholarship loan fund for young people who wanted to study to be atomic scientists.

First the sheriff could borrow from the fund, so he could go to college and learn to be an atomic scientist. Then, when he got a job, he could pay back the money. But the sheriff wouldn't need all the money. Other students could borrow from the fund too.

When Homer and Harry were ready to go to college, *they* could use the fund. Long ago, they had decided they were going to be atomic scientists when they grew up.

"Why!" Miss Pickerell said to herself, "it will be just like an atomic pile giving off energy to everything that is exposed to it! My scholarship will give an education to everybody who uses it."

The sheriff had got so interested in some easy atomic-energy books that Miss Pickerell had asked the state librarian to send to him, that he had already begun to like reading. He was very happy to be the first person to use Miss Pickerell's scholarship.

He gave up his sheriff job, went to college, and studied to be an atomic scientist.

The cave on Square Toe Mountain proved to be such a rich source of uranium, and there was so much of it, that for several years, uranium ore was mined there. It was still in operation when the sheriff finished college and became an atomic scientist.

He got his first job there, and boarded and roomed at Miss Pickerell's.

Miss Pickerell's cow continued in good health, and Miss Pickerell was pleased to see that the cow and the sheriff were developing quite an attachment for each other.

So many young students were helped by Miss Pickerell's scholarship, and they became such excellent atomic scientists, that the Atomic Energy Commission held a special ceremony in Miss Pickerell's honor.

All the scientists who had ever used Miss Pickerell's

scholarship were there. And they gave her a beautiful red leather autograph album, with all their autographs in it.

Homer and Harry always liked to look at the autograph album whenever they came to visit Miss Pickerell.

They knew that as soon as they became atomic scientists, Miss Pickerell would want their autographs in the album too.

BUILD YOUR OWN LIBRARY

Here are more Arrow Club books. Order them through your classroom club, or from Arrow Book Club, 33 West 42nd St., New York 36, N. Y.

If you order directly from Arrow Book Club please remember:

— to add 5 cents to the price of each book to cover handling and mailing

— that these prices apply only in the United States and its territories

— that payment *must* accompany your order.